Nightcat

CELESTA THIESSEN
KEZIAH THIESSEN

Join us in our adventure!
- Celesta Thiessen
- Keziah Thiessen

Cover art by Josh Branscum.

ISBN: 147741052X
ISBN-13: 978-1477410523

Printed in Canada

CONTENTS

CHAPTER 1 – THE SECRET OF THE NIGHT CATS

"But Mom, why do you have to leave?" asked Celesta. Celesta had blond curly hair and brown eyes. She was wearing her prettiest blue dress, to say goodbye to her parents. Celesta was one of three princesses. They were triplets - all seven years old, almost eight.

The whole family was standing inside the castle, near the large front doors.

"Because we are being overrun with dragons!" said the queen. Their mother had long brown ringlets and brown eyes.

All the children were very sad that their parents had to go. The king and queen had to find some way to stop the dragons. The children knew this quest could take their parents a long time.

"Why can't one of you stay?" asked Priscilla. Priscilla had beautiful, long brown hair, and she had brown eyes, like her sisters. She was wearing a lovely purple dress.

"Because," answered the king, "it would be too dangerous for one person to go alone. You will all be safe here, in Kitty Castle." Their father had brown eyes and short brown hair.

Kitty Castle was very old. It was a strong fortress. Some said there was magic deep within.

"Goodbye," moaned Keziah. She was afraid that her parents might get killed on such a dangerous trip. The dragon fire could burn anything except stone.

Everything else burned, even if it was raining! That's why it would be so dangerous for her parents. Keziah had curly, brown hair and dark brown eyes. She was wearing her most beautiful pink dress.

"Don't worry. Your tutor, Mr. Raymond, will help take care of you while we're gone," said the king.

"Nooo!" said David. "I don't think he even believes in dragons. He never goes outside. He never knows what's going on! How is *he* going to take care of us?" David had short blond hair and brown eyes. He was only five years old.

"Our cook, Daisy, will help him," said the king. "Don't worry. Everything will be fine."

"Richard, I want you to take care of your little sisters and brother, too," said their mother.

"I will, Mother," said Richard. Richard had short brown hair and brown eyes. He was eleven years old.

The king and queen then left. They slammed the door shut so that no dragon would get in and no cat would get out.

"Children," announced their tutor, "it is time for your studies." Mr. Raymond was a tall, skinny man with golden spectacles.

Sadly, the children walked up the stairs to the library. Their cat, whom they called Nightcat, came to greet them at the top of the stairs.

"Hi, Nightcat," Keziah said. They called their old, silver cat Nightcat because they had noticed that he stayed up all night, every night. They knew he was a very special cat. The children had noticed that many cats slept at nighttime but some cats stayed up all night. These were night cats and their pet was one of them.

Nightcat returned to the royal library where he liked to sleep because the cook had no interest in books - except cook books - and there were none of those in the library. Daisy kept the cookbooks in the kitchen. Daisy didn't like cats so Nightcat thought it best to keep away from her. He curled up on a pillow near the fireplace.

That night, the three sisters stayed up because they wanted to see what Nightcat did every night. They thought that he must be very lonely. As the sisters watched, Nightcat started down the winding staircase to the cellar. The princesses followed quietly behind the cat so that he wouldn't hear them. When they got to the basement, it was very dark. They couldn't see Nightcat. Then Keziah noticed something.

"Priscilla, Celesta, look!" whispered Keziah. "There's a secret passageway!" She pointed to an opening in the wall that was still partially open.

"Let's go in there," whispered Priscilla.

"I'm not so sure," said Celesta. "It looks pretty dark."

"I brought a flashlight, just in case," whispered Keziah.

"Good thinking!" said Celesta.

"Shhh...," whispered Keziah.

Keziah turned on her flashlight. They all went in. The passageway looked very old but they felt safe. Kitty Castle was their home. There was nothing to fear in Kitty Castle. Nightcat was far ahead of them. They hurried down the hallway to catch up. When they got to a large room, they found a small pool of water. Then they saw Nightcat. He seemed to be changing. He was growing! Something was happening to his back.

"Oh, no!" whispered Priscilla.

"I think it's okay," said Keziah.

Soon Nightcat was as big as a tiger and had large, silver-furred wings.

"It's the magic - the magic of Kitty Castle!" said Celesta.

"It's the magic we've been waiting for!" said Keziah.

Nightcat breathed and a few sparkles twinkled in the air. Then he turned and looked at the princesses.

"Nightcat, is that you?" asked Pricilla.

Then Nightcat spoke, "It is I! And this *is* the magic we've all been waiting for! Thank you for following me. You showed that you love me very much. It is your love that has turned me into the first good night cat in the world."

"Is there a way for us to stop the dragons now?" asked Keziah.

"Yes," answered Nightcat. "Dragons are night cats that have been treated badly. The cure is in this pool. My breath will put them to sleep and then you can splash this water on the dragons to turn them back into kittens."

"Well," said Keziah, "we must go to sleep now or we will get in trouble from our tutor." Mr. Raymond never let them stay up at night.

They tiptoed softly up to their room and went to bed.

In the morning, they awoke refreshed. It seemed like Nightcat had made the night last a little longer for them than for the others in the castle. When the brothers woke up, they were surprised to find that Nightcat was huge and had wings. They were scared, too. The sisters had to explain what had happened.

"I wouldn't believe it," said Richard, "if I didn't see it here with my own eyes."

"Thank you for never pulling my tail and for treating me with kindness," said

Nightcat to the boys. "You have helped me to change into a good night cat."

"Whoa," said David. "I didn't know you could talk!"

"It would be a good idea to keep quiet about me," said Nightcat. "The cook and your tutor don't like me. I think that I would frighten them."

"Okay," said Celesta.

"Now," said Nightcat, "I must go to sleep."

CHAPTER 2 – THE TROUBLED TUTOR

At breakfast, the children were all quiet. They didn't want the cook to hear them talking about Nightcat. But they knew they needed to talk. Finally, during their morning free time, they got their chance. They went up the winding stairs to their playroom in the high tower.

"I think we should tell Mr. Raymond," said Celesta.

"He won't believe you," said Keziah. "You'll just get in trouble."

"I'm not sure," said Richard. "Dad said he was supposed to be taking care of us. Maybe we should tell him."

"Well," said Priscilla, "we have Nightcat to take care of us now."

"Good point," said Keziah.

"I still think we should tell Mr. Raymond," Celesta insisted.

David said, "Remember what Nightcat said! We shouldn't tell about him."

"We should have a vote," Richard decided.

"I vote that we *shouldn't* tell about him," said Keziah. "What Nightcat said is probably true. He might frighten Mr. Raymond."

"Everyone who wants to tell Mr. Raymond, raise your hand," Richard told them.

Celesta raised her hand high in the air. She was the only one.

"Well, I still think we should tell," she exclaimed.

"We'll keep it a secret for now," said Richard. "We can always tell Mr. Raymond about Nightcat later."

"Oh!" said Keziah, "I hear Mr. Raymond calling us. We'd better hurry! He sounds worried."

They ran down the stairs.

"Maybe he saw Nightcat," whispered Keziah, as they hurried along.

When they got to the bottom of the stairs, they came out in the kitchen. Mr. Raymond looked very worried indeed.

"There's a bear in the castle!" Mr. Raymond exclaimed.

"See," said Celesta, "I told you we should tell him!"

"Tell me what?" asked their tutor, sternly.

"Nightcat has changed into a magical creature!" explained Priscilla.

"What!?" said Mr. Raymond. "This is serious."

"Nightcat is good, not bad!" said Keziah.

"Children, this isn't one of your games. Seriously! There is a bear in the castle!"

"It's not a bear!" cried Celesta. "It's Nightcat."

"If you children can't be serious, you should go straight back up to your playroom!"

"Okay," said David. The children turned around and headed back up the stairs.

"Make sure you close the door to your playroom!" called Mr. Raymond. "I don't want the bear to get you!"

"Okay," called Celesta.

On the way up, they stopped in the library, where their huge Nightcat was still sleeping.

"Nightcat," Keziah whispered.

Nightcat woke up.

"What?" he asked.

"I think Mr. Raymond saw you! He thinks you're a bear!" said Keziah.

"Oh, dear!" he exclaimed. "I'd better get out of sight!"

"You can sleep in our playroom," said Richard. "Mr. Raymond never goes up there. He says it's too messy. But I think he just doesn't like climbing all these stairs!"

Nightcat bounded up the stairs. The children followed behind him. They talked for a while but soon fell asleep. It was so cozy up there, with huge Nightcat purring as he slept.

Keziah woke up and looked out the window. It was already nighttime!

"Wake up! This is strange! We've missed our studies," said Keziah.

"Why didn't Mr. Raymond wake us up?" Priscilla asked.

"We need to go and find him!" said Richard.

"But what about Nightcat?" asked David, "Should we bring him?"

"I'm coming with you," said Nightcat. "I'll just make sure he doesn't see me."

They walked down the dark staircase. The children started their search in the library. Mr. Raymond was usually there.

"Maybe he just lost track of time," suggested Priscilla.

"I don't think so," said Keziah.

"Our tutor would never be so irresponsible," said Celesta.

Suddenly, Nightcat noticed a secret passageway. The door was partially open.

"Uh oh," said Nightcat.

"What?" asked the children.

"I see a secret passageway and the door is open. Maybe Mr. Raymond went in," said Nightcat.

"Why is that 'Uh oh'?" asked Richard.

"He's probably lost. That passage leads to the labyrinth beneath the castle," explained Nightcat. "I've been down there many times. There are lots of long and winding tunnels. It would be easy to get lost, but we won't get lost because I'll lead the way."

"I wonder why he went down there," Celesta said.

"I think he was probably looking for the bear," suggested David.

"So, let's go in, then," said Keziah.

They started down the dark tunnel, with Nightcat in the lead.

"Don't we need a flashlight or something?" whispered David.

"Why are you whispering?" asked Celesta.

“I’m not,” David said, overly loudly.

Celesta giggled.

“I like to keep one with me at all times, just in case,” Keziah said, flicking on a flashlight.

The beam shone weakly down the long tunnel.

“I still can’t see very much,” whined David.

“It’s okay,” said Nightcat, “I can see in the dark. I’ll take care of you.”

David patted his now lion-sized cat. They were all glad that Nightcat was there to take care of them.

“It’s possible he was following my paw prints,” explained Nightcat.

“Look,” said Keziah, “I see Mr. Raymond’s footprints in the dust!”

They followed the footprints for a long time, up one passageway and down another. After a while, they saw a faint light up ahead.

"That must be Mr. Raymond," said Nightcat softly. "You will need to take the lead now. I don't want to frighten him."

Richard took the flashlight from Keziah and took the lead. Soon they came to a very lonely-looking Mr. Raymond, sitting on the hard stone floor.

He said, "You shouldn't have come here! Now we're all lost!"

Richard began to laugh but then he quickly tried to stop. "It's pretty easy to find the way out," he told Mr. Raymond. "All we have to do is follow our footprints back."

Their tutor looked very embarrassed. "What smart thinking of you," he said to Richard.

"We're only so clever because we have a very good tutor," said Keziah.

Mr. Raymond smiled and Richard helped him up.

"It's good you brought a lantern," Keziah said to their tutor, still trying to help him feel better. "Our flashlight is almost out of batteries."

"Well," said Mr. Raymond, "I suggest we go immediately, before the bear finds us. I saw his terribly large footprints in these tunnels."

"We've missed our studies. Maybe we could do them now?" Keziah suggested.

Celesta glared at her in the dim light.

"I don't think so," said Mr. Raymond. "It has been a terrifying day. I'm exhausted. I'm sure you are as well. We shall all go straight to bed."

Keziah moaned.

CHAPTER 3 – THE WATER

When the children returned to their room, they found Nightcat waiting for them.

"Now," said Nightcat, "since you all have had a good sleep this afternoon, we can go adventuring."

"Okay!" Keziah replied quickly.

"What if Mr. Raymond sees you again?" asked David.

"That's the point," said Nightcat. "I need to learn how to be a normal cat in the daytime. I think it has something to do with that pool of water that is in the secret passage beyond the cellar."

"It's worth a try," said Priscilla.

"It's a good idea," said Richard. "We don't want another day like today."

"Here are some charged batteries," said Keziah. She replaced the batteries in her flashlight. "Let's go!"

The children followed Nightcat, tiptoeing softly so no one would hear them.

"Stop!" David said suddenly. "I think I hear something!"

Then they saw a light. It was coming from the kitchen.

"It must be Daisy, the cook," said Keziah.

"Shh...," whispered Richard.

"Let's get out of here," whispered Celesta.

"This way," said Nightcat. "There is another way down. I found it while I was exploring the castle." Nightcat led the children to a certain stone in the stairwell. There was a soft clicking sound and the wall swung inward. There were more stairs leading away.

"Let's hurry," whispered Richard. "Quietly! You know Daisy hates cats!"

The children followed their friend, Nightcat, into the tunnel. When the door was closed, Keziah flicked on her flashlight. Soon they found the large room with the pool of water in the middle.

Celesta said, "But I thought that this water will turn the dragons back into kittens?! We don't want to turn you back into a kitten!"

"I think Nightcat would be a cute kitten," giggled Priscilla.

"I don't think it will turn me back into a kitten," said Nightcat softly. "It only turns dragons into kittens if you splash it on to them. I think if I just take one lick, then I will be able to turn back into a regular cat for the day."

"Do you mean you will need to come and have a drink from this pool every day?" asked Celesta.

"No," Nightcat answered. "I believe that just one lick will make me able to control whether I'm a normal cat or in this form."

"So, drink," said Keziah, encouraging him.

The huge Nightcat leaned down to the water. Carefully, he put out his large tongue and lapped only once. Nothing happened.

"Why didn't anything happen?" asked David.

"I feel I'll be able to change back to my old self in the morning," said Nightcat. "That way I will be able to sleep in the library and not scare your tutor."

Nightcat looked at all the children fondly. "Thank you for coming with me. Even though I seem so much different now, I still need your love."

The children patted Nightcat fondly and they could hear a deep purr coming from his throat.

Suddenly, Keziah noticed the passageway seemed lighter. She flicked off her flashlight.

"I think it's almost morning," said Keziah. "We'd all better hurry back upstairs!"

"Let's pretend we're sleeping when we get back to our room," suggested David.

When they opened the door in the stairwell, light from a window shone down on Nightcat. Slowly, he began to shrink. His wings got shorter and then disappeared altogether into his soft fur. He was a normal cat again!

"Nightcat!" said Celesta.

But Nightcat just meowed. They had all stopped and were just staring at him.

"Let's get upstairs," said Keziah. "We don't want Mr. Raymond to find us here!"

The children hurried up to their room and jumped into their beds. Priscilla actually fell asleep in the few minutes that passed before Mr. Raymond came in to wake them up.

"Morning already?" asked Priscilla.

The children had breakfast and then they got straight to their studies. They had to work very hard since they had missed a day of school. It was a very busy morning. They even did an art project, using glue and pastels. Keziah made a picture of Nightcat.

After they had eaten lunch, their tutor looked at them with concern.

"You children don't seem well. Perhaps there was too much excitement yesterday, with a bear in the castle and all. Yes, I do believe we all had quite a scare. I think it would be best if we all had a little rest this afternoon."

The children all breathed a sigh of relief.

"Okay," said David.

"We did have a lot of excitement looking for you," said Richard.

"And we saw the creature face-to-face," said David.

Celesta scowled at her little brother.

"But we really did!" David whined.

"That's enough," said their tutor. "Now, off to your room."

They all lay down in their beds and quickly fell asleep. The next thing they knew, Daisy was waking them up for dinner.

"Time for dinner, Little Ones!" the cook called up the stairs. "I've made your favorite - pasta with cheese and chocolate cake for dessert!"

"Yes!" shouted David as he threw off his covers and headed down the stairs to the kitchen.

Celesta noticed that Nightcat was not in their room anymore. "Where's Nightcat?" she asked.

"Maybe he went into the secret passageway," whispered Richard. "Let's not talk about it in front of the cook."

The children sat at the large wooden table in the kitchen to have dinner. After dinner, their tutor, Mr. Raymond, read them a story. Then the children got free time.

"I think Nightcat is changing back to his other form!" said Keziah.

"Yes," said Priscilla, looking up at a high window. "It is getting dark outside."

"Maybe we should go to sleep," suggested Keziah. "That way we'll be ready for another night adventure."

"I want to go on an adventure now!" said David.

They all looked at the sky through the window.

"Maybe we could," said Richard, "if we were sure that Mr. Raymond and Daisy wouldn't notice. I wonder what Mr. Raymond is doing right now."

They could hear Daisy still working in the kitchen.

"I wonder what Nightcat is doing right now!" exclaimed David.

"I think he's waiting for us," suggested Celesta.

"We need to see where Mr. Raymond is," said Richard. "We don't want him to discover what we're up to."

"Good idea," replied Celesta.

"I'll go," said Richard. "You all wait here while I check it out."

The children waited anxiously for Richard to return. In a few minutes, he came back.

"He's already asleep!" Richard told them.

"Let's go find Nightcat!" said David impatiently.

"Wait! Which passageway do you think he went into?" asked Celesta.

"We can't go into the labyrinth ourselves. We could get lost!" said Keziah.

Then, suddenly, Nightcat came into their room. He was huge again and his wings looked even bigger than before.

CHAPTER 4 - REMEMBERING

"Nightcat," said the children, all running toward him. They hugged him and stroked his soft, silver fur.

"I'm so glad to see you," said Celesta.

"I'm so glad you're our cat," said David.

"Me too," said Nightcat.

"I remember when we first got you," said Richard.

"I don't remember that very well," said Keziah. "Could you tell us about it, Nightcat?"

"I was only a kitten, then," said Nightcat. "The dragons had started taking over the country. Great Aunt Esmeralda wanted to keep me safe because I was the youngest of all her cats. So she brought me here to Kitty Castle with some of her special things. We rode here on her fastest horse. Then she went back to her house for another load. She was going to bring the rest of her special things and the rest of her cats but she never returned. I never saw Great Aunt Esmeralda or my parents again."

"Aww…That's so sad," David said.

"Yes. I'm afraid Great Aunt Esmeralda might not have survived."

"I wonder what other things Great Aunt Esmeralda left here?" said Priscilla.

"And I wonder why they're so special," said Keziah.

"Were your parents magical nightcats like you are now?" asked Richard.

"No. They were just normal cats. I hope they survived. I wish I could see them again one day."

"Richard, what was it like when we first got Nightcat?" asked Celesta.

"It was great," said Richard. "We'd never had a cat before."

"When he was a kitten, he used to sleep in my bed. That was five years ago. I was six and you princesses were three and David was only just born."

"That's why *I* don't remember it," said David.

"Even I can hardly remember back then," said Keziah.

"Do you remember Great Aunt Esmeralda?" asked Priscilla.

"I remember that she had lots of cats!" said Keziah.

"I sort of remember her," said Richard. "She had green eyes and curly white hair."

"Was she nice?" asked Celesta

"Yes," said Richard. "She was very nice."

"Do you remember what her special things were?" asked Keziah.

"No," said Richard. "I don't remember."

"I don't remember much about her special things either," said Nightcat. It's hard to remember because I was so young."

"Was it scary riding on horseback to the castle, when the dragons were starting to come?"

"Yes," said Nightcat. "The dragons were overhead and they were swooping at us."

"Were the dragons the same as they are now? What was it like to live here before the dragons came?" asked Priscilla.

"The dragons were smaller at first and so they weren't as dangerous. They used to be all cat-sized."

"It was nice before the dragons came," said Richard. "You could go outside and play whenever you wanted to. I used to have lots of friends who lived in the village. But now I never see them anymore."

"And we used to have flowers in front of the castle; I remember that," said Celesta.

"And grass," said Keziah, "and trees."

"The only place trees grow now is in our courtyard because the dragons can't get there," said Priscilla.

"And in the glass greenhouses," said Richard. "That's where the farmers grow food now, so the dragons can't burn it."

"I think I have a photo album up on the top shelf in my closet," said Celesta.

"I've always loved history," said Keziah, "but this is way more fun."

"Let's get it!" said Richard.

They went to Celesta's closet but the children couldn't reach the album because it was too high up.

"Fly up and get it!" David said to Nightcat.

"Just climb up on my back, Richard," suggested Nightcat. "Then you'll be able to reach it."

Richard climbed up on Nightcat's back and got the photo album.

"How exciting!" said Celesta. "Let's look inside."

They opened the photo album.

"Whoa!" said David. "Grass was green? I thought it was brown!"

The princesses and Richard laughed.

"Only dead or burned grass is brown," said Keziah.

The first photograph was of Richard playing outside.

"Whoa!" said David. "What's that?" he asked pointing to a picture of flowers.

"They're trolls," said Richard.

"No!" said Keziah. "They're flowers! I have some dried flowers pressed in a book. Let me show you!" Keziah wandered off to her room.

"You're right," said David. "It used to be very pretty outside."

"Yeah," said Priscilla. "I miss playing outside."

Then Keziah returned with her flowers.

"These are my favorite flowers," she said, pointing to dried snapdragons.

"Can I touch them?" asked David.

"Sure," said Keziah. "Just be careful. They can break."

David touched the faded, dried flowers.

"I hope flowers can grow outside again one day," said Celesta.

"Oh, look," said Nightcat, staring at the next photograph. "It's Aunt Esmeralda!"

The children all crowded around to see.

"And she's wearing a tiara," said Keziah. "I wonder if that is one of the special things that she left here."

"It might be," said Nightcat. "She would often wear it or keep it close to her."

They flipped the page.

"Awww...It's you as a kitten, Nightcat," said Priscilla.

"You were so cute," said Celesta.

"It's getting late," said Richard. "Let's put the photo album away."

"Nightcat, just fly up and tuck it back onto the top shelf."

"I have a problem," Nightcat admitted.

"What is it?" asked Keziah, looking and sounding very worried.

"I don't know how to fly."

CHAPTER 5 – THE PROBLEM WITH NIGHTCAT

"Oh, no!" said Celesta. "How do you know you can't fly?"

"I tried it out in the courtyard. I fell."

"I don't know if we will be able to help you," said Richard.

"Maybe we can teach you," suggested Keziah.

"It's worth a try," said Nightcat. "I won't be able to fight the dragons if I can't fly."

They all went down the stairs very quietly. Then they opened the door to the courtyard. The courtyard was surrounded by the castle on all sides. The dragons could not get into the courtyard because the castle walls were very, very high. No one ever came out into the courtyard. It was just trees and weeds and cobble stone pavement. They were sure no one would see them. Richard was careful to close the door behind them.

"Why don't you show us what you can do," suggested Richard.

"Okay," said Nightcat.

He stretched out his wide silver wings and flapped. Nothing happened. He flapped and flapped and flapped. Dust flew up into the air all around him but Nightcat did not move.

"Maybe you're too fat," said David.

"David!" said Celesta. "Don't say that!"

"Don't worry," said Priscilla to Nightcat. "You're not too fat!"

"Maybe you should try jumping," suggested Keziah.

"I don't know anything," sobbed Nightcat. "I thought I could fight the dragons and now I can't even fly!"

"Awww...," said Priscilla. She patted his large, furry head.

"You'll learn to fly eventually," said Keziah. "Sometimes it takes birds a while but they do learn!"

"Jumping sounds like a good idea," said Richard, also petting their huge cat. "You were always a very good jumper."

"That's true." Nightcat sniffed. "I am a good jumper. I'll try."

"Now you'll be a double good jumper," said David, "because you're twice as big!"

Nightcat crouched down and then sprung up in the air, a blur of sliver fur. He flapped a few times and then landed back on his feet.

"Try again," said Richard.

"Try running first," suggested Priscilla.

Nightcat ran across the yard and jumped, flapping his wings furiously. At first, it looked as if he were going to fall, but then, as the children cheered him on, he started flying. He turned in the air and made the short flight back to them.

Nightcat landed beside the children. They all rushed to him and stroked his silky fur.

"You did it!" cried Priscilla.

"I knew you could do it!" said Keziah.

"Thank you for believing in me," said Nightcat.

"What else can you do?" asked Priscilla.

"Can you breathe fire?" asked David.

"Of course not!" said Celesta. "He would burn his fur!"

"I think I should be able to breathe sparkle dust," said Nightcat. "Here. Let me try it."

Nightcat took a deep breath. Then he blew a long blast of warm air. No sparkle dust.

"Try again, Nightcat," said Richard. "It worked last time when you kept trying."

"I know you can do it!" said Celesta.

Nightcat took another deep breath. He looked at the children. He thought about how he had to be able to fight the dragons in order to save all the people of the kingdom. As he breathed out, sparkles flew everywhere!

Keziah was standing nearest to him. She stepped back quickly, hoping none of the sparkle dust had hit her. She knew that, since Nightcat was magic, the sparkle dust would be magic too. Luckily, none of the children had breathed in any of the sparkles.

"I did it!" cried Nightcat.

"What happens if you breathe that on someone?" asked Priscilla.

"They'll fall asleep for a long time," answered Nightcat. "And the water from the pool will turn the dragons back into kittens."

"Try flying again," said Celesta.

"Yes," said Richard, "you need to practice your skills."

Nightcat flew low around the courtyard at first. Then he flew higher and higher. The children cheered and cheered. Nightcat circled the yard, getting higher each time. Then, with one final pounce, Nightcat pushed himself over the castle wall.

"Nightcat!" gasped Celesta.

"Oh, no!" moaned Priscilla. "The dragons will get him!"

"I can't believe Nightcat made it over the wall," said Richard. "Even the dragons can't do that."

"It's because Nightcat is *way* better than a dragon," said David.

"But what about the fire the dragons make?" asked Priscilla.

"He won't get hurt," said David. "He's too smart for that!"

"He will probably come back in the morning," said Keziah.

"Right," said Richard. "I know that we will see Nightcat again very soon."

"We might as well go to bed," said Celesta.

Quietly the children returned to their room to wait for morning and for Nightcat.

KITTY CASTLE BOOKS

Get all the Kitty Castle books on Amazon.com!

KITTY CASTLE 1 - NIGHTCAT

KITTY CASTLE 2 - SURPRISES!

KITTY CASTLE 3 - ANSWERS!

KITTY CASTLE 4 - MYSTERY!

KITTY CASTLE 5 - REUNION

If you liked this book, please leave us a great review on Amazon.com! Thanks for reading!